MW01680310

The Three Little Pigs Wise Up

and

The Princess, the Prince, and the Vegetables

by Alan Kramer
illustrated by Amy Vangsgard

The Three Little Pigs Wise Up

Place: Office of the architects Designit and Buildit

Characters: Buildit, Mary Mary, Designit, the Three Little Pigs, the Big Bad Wolf

(The Three Little Pigs sit in chairs, reading magazines and waiting their turn to see the Architects. Finally, a door opens, and the Architects enter, talking with Mary Mary.)

Buildit: (*He's already said this a million times.*) Mary Mary. We keep trying to explain. We can't help you with this.

Mary Mary: (*pleading*) But my garden! You can't believe how it grows!

Designit: Yes, we can. You told us over and over and over already.

Mary Mary: (*reciting the poem*) With cockle shells! And silver bells!

Buildit and Designit: (*together*) And pretty maids all in a row!! We know! We know!

Mary Mary: But you have to help me. What I wanted to plant was corn!!

Designit: Mary Mary, we know how you feel. But we can't help you.

Buildit: We design buildings! We don't do gardens.

Designit: You need a landscape architect.

Buildit: Or a farmer.

Buildit and Designit: (*together*) NEXT!!!

(*Mary storms off in a huff.*)

Buildit: (*to the Three Little Pigs*) She's quite contrary, you know.

Pig #1: Contrary?

Buildit and Designit: (*together, quoting from the poem*) "Mary, Mary quite contrary, how does your garden grow?"

Three Pigs: (*together*) Ahhhh.

Designit: May we help you, Mr.— (*waiting for the Pigs to introduce themselves*)

Pig #1: Pig.

Pig #2: Pig.

Pig #3: Pig.

(*They all shake hands, saying their names at the same time.*)

Buildit and Designit: (*together*) How can we help you?

Pig #1: We have a wolf problem.

Buildit and Designit: (*together*) Hmmmm.

Buildit: What kind of wolf problem?

Pig #2: Every time we build a house, this wolf comes along…

Designit: What kind of wolf exactly? There are different kinds, you know.

Pig #3: A Big Bad Wolf.

Buildit: I see. Go on. What does he do?

Pig #1: He blows our houses down.

Buildit and Designit: (*together*) Ahhhh.

Pig #2: It's terrible.

Buildit: (*writing down notes*) Exactly how does he do this?

Pig #3: First he huffs.

Pig #1: Then he puffs.

Pig #2: And then he blows them down.

Designit: Blows down your houses?

Pig #3: He has very strong lungs.

Buildit: Do you know why he does this?

Pig #1: No. He bangs on the door and tells us we have to let him in.

Pig #2: Then, when we don't, he goes into the huffing and puffing business.

Pig #3: It's very upsetting.

Pig #1: What can we do?

Designit: What kind of houses do you have?

Pig #3: Mine's made out of straw.

Buildit: Straw? Plain ordinary straw?

Pig #3: It's all natural, all-American straw. I collected it myself. What's the matter with straw?

Designit: Even I could blow down a house made out of straw. (*Pig #3 sits down, hurt.*)

Pig #2: (*proudly*) Mine is made out of sticks.

Buildit: Sticks? What kind of sticks?

Pig #2: Mostly popsicle sticks. I tried licorice sticks, cinnamon sticks, and sticks of gum, but every time I turned my back someone had eaten a piece of my house. It was very frustrating.

Designit: (*amazed*) Popsicle sticks?? You built your house out of popsicle sticks??

Pig #2: What's wrong with that?

Designit: If you want to keep out wolves, you have to do better than popsicle sticks! (*Pig #2 sits down, hurt.*)

Pig #1: My house is made out of bricks.

Buildit: (*curious*) Bricks? What kind?

Pig #1: (*holding up a brick, as in a TV commercial*) The best quality red brick, with double reinforced steel things inside and stuff mixed in for an extra strong anti-wolf support.

Designit: Well, that's more like it!

Buildit: You guys should move in with him.

Pig #1: But there isn't enough room.

Designit: Ah. That's where we can help you.

Buildit: All of our buildings meet the strict standards of the American Anti-Huffing-and-Puffing Society.

Designit: Do you want to see our seal of approval?

Pig #2: No, thank you.

Pig #3: So what should we do?

Designit: You need a new house! I have one right here. It should give the three of you plenty of room. (*He unrolls a big picture of the Empire State Building.*)

Pig #2: (*shocked*) What is that?!?

Pig #3: That's not a house.

Buildit: (*talking to Designit and ignoring the Pigs*) They don't need a new house! They need an addition on their brick house. We can add on to the back and put an extra room over the garage. And they MUST have a moat!

(*He holds up a picture of Pig #1's house with an ugly addition and a moat with sharks swimming in the water.*)

Pig #1: What did you do to my house?!?

Designit: An addition won't work! They need a whole new house!!

Buildit: No! They need an addition!!

(Buildit and Designit argue back and forth, yelling "A new house!" and "An addition!" at each other. They exit, leaving the Three Little Pigs alone. The Big Bad Wolf enters. The Pigs see the Wolf and hold onto each other in fear.)

Wolf: Relax. Relax. It's okay.

Pig #1: Okay? No, it's not! Whatever it is, it's definitely not okay!!

Wolf: I won't hurt you. I promise.

Pig #2: You expect us to believe that?!

Pig #3: You tried to eat us!

Wolf: Me? Eat you? I did no such thing! (*proudly*) I'm a vegetarian.

Pig #1: A vegetarian?

Wolf: I only eat salads. And broccoli. Lots of broccoli. And spinach. I love spinach!

Pig #2: No pork?

Wolf: No meat of any kind.

Pig #3: Then why did you blow our houses down?

Wolf: I asked you nicely if I could come in, but all you said was "not by the hair on my chinny-chin-chin." (*almost crying*) You hurt my feelings.

Pig #3: That doesn't give you the right to blow a house down.

Wolf: (*embarrassed*) I'm sorry. You're right. That wasn't very nice.

Pig #2: If you didn't want to eat us, what did you want?

Wolf: I wanted to offer you a special deal on the all-new *Fairytale Characters Encyclopedia*. Want to see it?

(The Pigs look at each other and shrug. The Wolf pulls out a copy of the book and shows them the pictures.)

Wolf: You see? (*to Pig #1*) There's you. (*Pig #1 squeals with delight.*) And you. (*Pig #2 squeals.*) And you. (*Pig #3 squeals.*)

Pig #1: Why don't you come over to my house, and we can look at the rest of it there. (*They start to walk off together.*)

Wolf: If you buy a set this month, you get the CD-ROM version for free.

Three Pigs: Wow!

(*They exit, just as the Architects re-enter, holding a big picture of Disneyworld.*)

Buildit and Designit: (*together*) We've got it!! Your new home!!!

(*They look around for the Pigs. Not seeing them, they shrug.*)

Buildit and Designit: (*together*) NEXT!!

The Princess, The Prince, and The Vegetables

Place: Inside a castle

Characters: The Princess, the King, the Queen, Prince Charming

Princess: (*calling from offstage*) Hello! Excuse me! Could I get a little help here? Hey!! (*Finally, she staggers onstage holding an enormous papier-mâché pea.*) Somebody! Please!!!

King: (*in his bedclothes, rubbing his eyes*) What? What's the matter? It's the middle of the night. (*Together, they finally manage to put the pea down.*)

Princess: Thank you.

King: So what's the problem?

Princess: (*impatient*) Is this how you treat all your guests? This was in my bed.

King: (*moving closer*) What is it?

Princess: I don't know, but it weighs a ton! I haven't slept a wink.

King: Try counting sheep. (*He turns and starts to leave.*)

Princess: Hey! (*He stops.*)

King: What is it now?

Princess: There's more.

King: More?

Princess: More vegetables. (*The Queen enters, fully dressed. She's been awake.*)

Queen: (*excited*) Ah. I see you found it!

Princess: Found what?

Queen: The tiny little pea I placed under all the soft mattresses in your bed.

Princess: The tiny what?

Queen: The teeny tiny little pea I placed under the guest-room mattresses before you went to sleep. Only a true princess could feel such a teeny tiny little thing. (*There's a long moment of silence.*)

Princess: (*rolling the huge pea up to her*) You mean this?

Queen: Yes.

Princess: Are you serious? Number one, this is no teeny tiny little anything. If this is a pea, it should be in the *Guinness Book of Records.* Number two, what soft mattresses? You told me you had sent all your mattresses out to be cleaned. You made me sleep on a piece of wood on the floor. This teeny tiny little thing was nailed to the middle of it.

King: Nailed?

Princess: Along with bunches of broccoli...

King: Broccoli?

Princess: Some artichokes...

King: Artichokes?

Princess: And a pile of Brussels sprouts.

King: Yuck! (*turning on the Queen*) What were you trying to do?

Queen: (*to the King*) You know very well what I was doing. It was a test.

Princess: A test?

Queen: When you knocked on the door last night, I thought maybe you were a princess. But I couldn't be sure. I had to test you. Only a true princess would be so brave. So strong. So honest. So understanding of vegetables. (*Turning to the King*) I think she's perfect.

Princess: Perfect? For what?

Queen: To marry our son, the prince.

Princess: To do what??

Queen: To marry Prince Charming, our only son and heir to the throne.

Princess: (*turning and heading for the door*) Good-bye!

King: No. Wait! (*She stops.*)

Princess: Why should I marry this prince?

King: (*to the Queen*) Tell her why.

Queen: Because he's our son. And a prince. And very charming. And a prince.

King: You told her that already.

Princess: And...? And what else?

Queen: (*looking afraid to answer*) And we have to find a princess to marry him right away.

Princess: And why do you have to find a princess to marry him right away? (*She turns to the King for the answer.*)

King: The Queen is in charge of answers.

Princess: OK. (*turning back to the Queen*) Why do you need a princess to marry him?

Queen: (*to the King*) Should I tell her?

King: If you don't, she's going to try to leave again.

Queen: She can't. I nailed the doors shut.

Princess: (*She can't take it anymore.*) Please! Tell me! Now!

Queen: (*She turns and calls sweetly, offstage.*) Darling! Oh, Prince! Prince Charming! Hello! Oh, Prince Charming!

Prince Charming: (*sleepily calling from offstage*) What is it?

Queen: Your mommy is calling you!

Prince Charming: (*staggering on in his bedclothes; he's a frog!*) Mother! What? What is it? Why are you calling me? It's the middle of the night!

Princess: Who is this?

King: Why, Prince Charming, of course.

Princess: But he's a frog!

Prince Charming: Who are you?

Princess: I'm a princess.

Prince Charming: (*turning angrily to the Queen*) Mother! Not another one!

Queen: The others weren't real princesses, my darling. That was the problem. This one is a real princess. She knew the names of all the vegetables!

Prince Charming: Even the Brussels sprouts?

Queen: Even the Brussels sprouts.

Prince Charming: (*to the Princess*) I love vegetables.

Princess: I thought frogs ate flies.

Prince Charming: Yuck!!! I'm a green frog. I like anything that's green. That's why I can jump so well. Do you want to see me jump?

Princess: No, thank you.

Queen: Now, don't you go jumping again, Charming. That's no way for a Prince to behave.

Prince Charming: But I'm a frog, Mother! F-r-o-g, frog. Frogs jump. I like to jump. I like being a frog.

King: (*correcting*) You're a prince who has been turned into a frog.

Queen: A wizard put a spell on you.

Prince Charming: (*explaining for the millionth time*) No. I'm just a regular frog. The wizard put the spell on you. It turned your brain into applesauce. You think I'm a prince. But I'm not!

Princess: This is very confusing.

Prince Charming: You're telling me!?

Queen: Now, Princess. All our son needs is for a real princess—that's you!—to kiss him, and he'll turn back into our own dear Prince Charming.

Princess: Do I have to kiss him on the lips?

Queen: No. A nice little kiss on the top of his head will do fine.

Princess: I don't know.

Prince Charming: Mother. I've had enough of princesses and kissing. Please!!

Queen: But, Charming, the other princesses weren't real princesses. This time it will work. I promise you.

Prince Charming: But I don't want to be a prince! How many times do I have to tell you that?

Princess: Wait! I have an idea. I'll kiss him. But if he doesn't turn into a prince, you have to promise to let him be a frog.

Queen: (*not sure*) I don't know about this.

Princess: It's either that, or I'm not kissing anyone. (*The Queen and King whisper about this a minute.*)

King: All right. But it better be a real kiss.

Princess: I promise.

(*The Princess kisses Charming's forehead. Charming covers his eyes. Everyone stands absolutely still for a long moment. Nothing happens.*)

Prince Charming: (*jumping for joy*) Yes! Yes!! I'm a frog! I'm a frog!! (*The Queen almost faints, and the King helps her off. To the Princess:*) Thank you so much!

Princess: You're welcome. I'm glad I could help. Now I have a favor to ask you.

Prince Charming: Anything. Just name it.

Princess: Until a wizard came and cast a spell on me, I used to be a cocker spaniel. Do you think you could help me?

Prince Charming: Absolutely. Should I kiss you on the forehead, too?

Princess: It's worth a try. (*He kisses her. As soon as he does, the Princess starts barking like a cocker spaniel and jumping around happily.*) Woof! Woof! I'm free! I'm free! (*She runs off, jumping and barking.*)

Prince Charming: (*smiling at the audience*) Ribbit. (*He hops off.*)